THE FRANKENSTEIN JOURNALS

Written by Scott Sonneborn

raintree

a Capstone company — publishers for children

Raintree is an imprint of Capstone Global Library Limited, a company incorporated in England and Wales having its registered office at 7 Pilgrim Street, London, EC4V 6LB – Registered company number: 6695582

www.raintree.co.uk
myorders@raintree.co.uk

Text and illustrations © Capstone Global Library Limited 2016
The moral rights of the proprietor have been asserted.

Printed and bound in China.

ISBN 978 1 4747 0740 4

19 18 17 16 15
10 9 8 7 6 5 4 3 2 1

British Library Cataloguing in Publication Data
A full catalogue record for this book is available from the British Library.

Every effort has been made to contact copyright holders of material reproduced in this book. Any omissions will be rectified in subsequent printings if notice is given to the publisher.

Designed by Hilary Wacholz

Cover artwork and illustrations by Timothy Banks

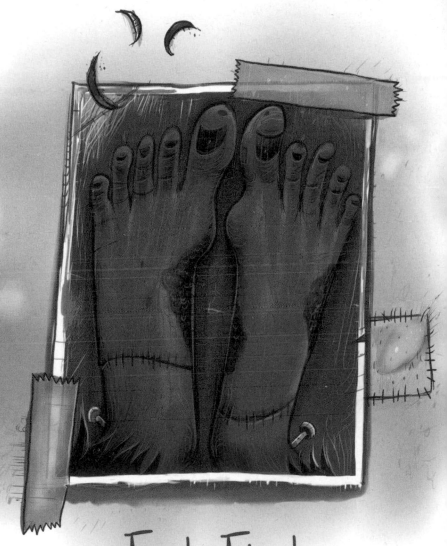

Feet First

Chapter 1

BORRRRING. That's how I'd describe the first (13) years of my life. Don't get me wrong ... living at Mr Shelley's Orphanage for Lost and Neglected Children wasn't ALWAYS bad. But, more often than not, life was just a big old helping of boredom.

Thankfully, Year #14 made up for it all. Which is why I'm writing this journal. Because Year #14 needs to be remembered (or at least not forgotten).

So, in case you were wondering, my future self, here's what you looked like then...

I'VE GOT STYLE!

Hmm ... you know, looking back, I can see why I never got adopted. I suppose I made an odd first impression. Something about me just doesn't quite match. Or, actually, a lot of things don't:

1. My right eye is blue and my left is green.

2. I have short fingers on one hand and long ones on the other.

3. One leg is longer than the other.

4. My feet are much too big for my legs (not to mention two completely different sizes!).

VERY ANNOYING!

5

Sure, not everyone noticed these "qualities" the first time they saw me. But anyone who spent time with me, for example, trying to decide if they wanted to take me home, saw them eventually.

Growing up at Mr Shelley's Orphanage for Lost and Neglected Children, I thought a lot about being part of a family. I used to daydream all the time that somewhere out there I had the HUGEST family in the world. But Mr Shelley, the head of the orphanage, never discovered who left me there. Mr Shelley always told me that he found me lying on a blanket in a box.

He called me John Doe ... JD for short.

Although I wasn't the greatest orphan, Mr Shelley would be the first to tell you that he wasn't the greatest head of an orphanage. Mr Shelley was having a hard time getting enough donations and volunteers, and now the orphanage was in trouble.

In fact, the orphanage would have to close down. All the other orphans had found homes. It was just me who was left.

One day, Mr Shelley got a letter. The energy company said they'd be turning off the power supply sometime in the next 24 hours.

And that's when this monster mystery started...

"That'll do it," said Mr Shelley from inside his office. "I suppose this is the last time I'll see this place. Or it would be, if I could see anything with all the lights off!"

I went into his office and handed him a torch.

"Thank you, JD," said Mr Shelley. "I really don't know what I'd do without you. But I suppose I am about to find out."

"I'm sorry I couldn't do better for you," he said, the corners of each eye springing a tear. "Sorry I couldn't find you a family. Sorry I failed at yet another job.

Sorry I have to move to Las Vegas and work in my brother-in-law's ice cream van."

Mr Shelley shivered at the thought.

"Don't panic, sir," I told him. "I'll work something out. I promise."

MR SHELLEY

"You always say that," said Mr Shelley. "And you always do it, too. Without you, this orphanage would have fallen apart a long time ago. I always said you were my right-hand man."

He had always said that. I had always thought that was strange, because my LEFT hand is much bigger and stronger than my RIGHT.

"You were the one keeping this place going," he continued. "It's probably better for you that we go our separate ways. But before we do..."

Mr Shelley used the torch to find a box under his desk.

"The bank is going to repossess the building and everything in it. We're only allowed to take our personal belongings. This is yours," Mr Shelley said, putting the box on his desk. "This is the box I found you in outside the orphanage."

The only thing inside the box was a blanket.

"You were lying on that when I found you at the door," said Mr Shelley proudly. "You never forget your first orphan. I remember it like it was yesterday."

I couldn't say I remembered that, but then, I was just a baby. I picked up the blanket to take a closer look. The blanket smelled musty and old.

I let out a violent sneeze.

"Oh my!" exclaimed Mr Shelley.

"Don't worry," I shrugged. "It's just my allergies."

But Mr Shelley wasn't looking at me. He was gaping at the bottom of the box. Underneath where the blanket had been was a book.

"Well, what do you know!" exclaimed Mr Shelley. "I never even thought to look under the blanket."

I opened the book. It was a journal (a bit like the one I'm writing in now). But someone had already filled all the pages of this one. And as I flicked through them, a photograph fell out. It must have been stuck in between the pages. I picked it up.

It was a photo of a baby being held by ...

FRANKENSTEIN'S MONSTER!

Not that there's anything strange about that. I had seen plenty of photos of Frankenstein's Monster.

A while ago (it may have been ten years – or no, it was almost fifteen years ago) Frankenstein's Monster made a BIG SPLASH in the news before disappearing without a trace. No one had seen or heard from him since.

From what I remembered reading about him, Frankenstein's Monster hadn't been a bad sort of monster. (Not like the Mummy – that monster left a big mess in the middle of our town a couple of years ago!)

On the back of the photo was a note:

One day, you'll know why I had to leave forever. But I want you to have this so you'll know where you came from.

Love, Dad

I looked at the baby again. Even though he couldn't have been more than a couple of months old, I could see that one of the baby's legs was shorter than the other. His left hand was much bigger than his right. And he had one green eye and one blue one.

That baby was me!

My dad was Frankenstein's MONSTER!

MY DAD

Chapter 2

WELL, THAT EXPLAINED A LOT!!

Like why one of my eyes was blue and the other bright green. Why one hand was big with long fingers, the other small with short, stubby ones. Why both my feet were much too big for my legs.

They all came from different parts of different people that went into my father!!

It was a lot to take in all at once. For thirteen years, I hadn't known anything about my family.

And now...

It was like discovering your dad was a king or a famous rock star. Only mine was a monSTAR!

But it gave me an idea.

I had always dreamed of having a big family. So, my dad was gone. And I didn't know if I'd ever had a mum. But that didn't mean I didn't have a family out there. Parts from lots of people went Into my dad. All those people were a part of him, and he passed their hands, feet, eyes and hands to me.

Which meant the people who went into him were sort of related to me. I thought those people were probably all dead. (At least, I hoped they had been dead before their legs, arms and feet were taken from them to make my dad!) (GROSS!)

But those people whose parts went into my dad ... they probably had relatives who were still alive. I was related to them, too. They were like my cousins!

Which meant, somewhere out there, the thing I'd spent years daydreaming about was actually true! I had a MONSTER family! A family made up of the descendants of the dozens of people whose parts made up Frankenstein's Monster.

All I had to do was track down where each part of my dad came from to find them!

I said all this to Mr Shelley as we stood there in his office, looking at Dr Frankenstein's journal with the torch.

The journal was made up of hundreds of pages of notes, scribbles, drawings and maps. It didn't have an index, or a glossary, or whatever else you call those parts of books that tell you where to find what you're looking for inside.

I had no idea where to start.

"How about at the beginning?" suggested Mr Shelley, pointing to the cover.

DUH!

If found, please
return to

Dr. Victor Von Frankenstein,
423 Greenbush Avenue

Chapter 3

First thing the next morning, Mr Shelley dropped me off on his way to Las Vegas. He had been very relieved that I had somewhere to go. Mr Shelley's brother-in-law had insisted there was room in his ice cream van for only one more, and Mr Shelley didn't want to argue with him. I couldn't blame him. From what I had overheard of their phone conversations, his brother-in-law sounded pretty tough for an ice cream man.

I said goodbye and thanked Mr Shelley for everything, including the lift.

Having lived my whole life in the same room at the orphanage, I didn't have a lot of experience when it came to finding my way to new places.

When Mr Shelley drove off, I forgot to breathe for a minute. What if this didn't work? What if I never found my family? What if they didn't want me to find them? And how could the head of an orphanage leave a kid behind without even waiting to see what happened to me?

Actually, the answer to the last question was pretty obvious. Mr Shelley never was very good at his job. He was pretty hopeless, in fact.

"Don't panic," I told myself, the way I'd told Mr Shelley a thousand times. "You'll work something out."

CREEPY!!

I double-checked the address to make sure I was in the right place. But I already knew that I was. Every house in the road looked the same. Except this one.

This one looked like a HAUNTED CASTLE.

I knocked on the door. A minute later, a voice came from inside: "Yes?"

"Um ... is this the Frankenstein residence?" I asked, hoping I didn't sound as nervous as I was.

"Yes," answered a muffled voice through the door.

I wondered if Dr Frankenstein would be some kind of scary mad scientist with wild hair? Or a nice old man who wanted to help me?

As the door began to open, I tried to be ready for anyone or ANYTHING.

FRAN

I certainly wasn't ready for what I finally saw.

Holding the door open was a GIRL who was maybe three years older than me. "This better be important," she said. "You're interrupting a moment of brilliant insight."

MY FIRST CRUSH!

"Oh," was all I could think to say.

I had been expecting some old scientist, not a teenage girl. It didn't help that she was really pretty, too.

"Okay then," she said, starting to shut the door.

"Wait!" I said. "I'm here to see Dr Frankenstein."

That got her to stop closing the door slowly.

Instead, she slammed it shut – **BANG!!**

"No one by that name lives here!" she shouted through the thick door.

"But, but –" I pleaded. "You said this was the Frankenstein residence!"

She opened the door slightly.

"I must have misheard you," she said, looking down her nose. "This door is very thick. I thought you said the Fran Kenstein residence."

"Right," I nodded. "Frankenstein."

The name made her shudder. "No," she said, annoyed. "Fran Kenstein. My name is Frances Kenstein. There is no Frankenstein here!"

"Oh," was all I could think to say again.

I felt as though someone had jumped on my stomach and pushed all the air out.

If this was a dead end, I didn't know where to look next.

"Are you ill?" she asked. "Something about you looks a little ... off."

"Oh, no, that's just me," I said. "I get my looks from my dad," I added proudly.

"I must have made a mistake," I told her, picking up my bag to go. Although I had no idea where I'd go. "It's just, I found this journal, and it said –"

I reached into my bag, past my own journal, and pulled out Dr Frankenstein's.

As soon as I did, her eyes lit up. As though there was a glittering torch inside each one.

They actually sort of sparkled. (Give me a break. I said she was pretty, didn't I?)

"Why didn't you say so!" she exclaimed as she grabbed my big left hand and dragged me inside the house. "Come in!"

It was the **FIRST TIME** I had ever held hands with a girl.

Fran sat me down in her kitchen and offered me anything I wanted from her fridge. When I opened it, the only thing I saw inside was a big bowl of GUACAMOLE.

"Sorry if I was rude before," she said as she placed the bowl of green stuff in front of me. I was hungry, but I wasn't sure how to eat it. There didn't seem to be any crisps.

"Dr Frankenstein was my father," she told me. "But I'm so sick of hearing his name. I'm tired of people comparing me to him. I'm a brilliant scientist myself, you know. I was in the middle of an AMAZINGLY challenging experiment when you knocked on the front door."

"Oh," I said, impressed. She was pretty AND smart!

"I want to be my own person and do great things of my own without people always thinking of Dr Frankenstein when they hear my name," she said. "You can understand that, can't you?"

"Definitely," I nodded, because it seemed like the right thing to say. But actually I didn't really understand. Nobody had ever thought of my dad when they heard my name. Mostly because, until today, nobody – including me – knew who my dad even was.

"So that's why I changed my name," she said.

"To Fran Kenstein?" I asked.

"Exactly." She nodded as if that made perfect sense. She took a bite of guacamole. Which wasn't as easy as it sounds without any crisps. Or even a spoon!

"I've lived alone in this house since my father died," she said, pointing at the kitchen and the large house beyond. "Doing my own experiments. Which are really quite brilliant."

"But enough about me." She smiled, and then gave me a serious look. "Let's talk about my father's journal! I had no idea where it was. Your dad must have stolen it. He and my father never really got along very well."

"Hey, wait a minute!" I said, but then stopped short.

I was about to stick up for my dad. But then I thought, maybe he did steal Dr Frankenstein's journal. I didn't know him well enough to be sure he wouldn't do something like that (he was a MONSTER, after all). And Fran seemed certain that he had.

Suddenly, I realized something else.

HMMMMMM...

"Wait, did you know my dad?" I asked excitedly. "What was he like? Did you know my mum? Do I even have a mum?"

I had a million more questions. But Fran stopped me before I could get any of them out.

"There's so much I can tell you," Fran said. "But first we should get to work on finding out whose body parts were used to make your father!"

I couldn't believe it. I hadn't even told her why I had come here, and she was going to help me do it!

Did I mention she was pretty, too?

Fran asked if she could see her father's journal. I reached into my bag and pulled out a book.

"WHOOPS! That's my journal," I said, stuffing it back into my bag. "Here's your dad's."

Fran took it and started scanning the pages into her computer on the kitchen table.

"Once the pages are scanned, it will be easy to cross-reference and find whom each part of the monster came from," she explained.

I felt that happy tingling in the back of my shoulders I only felt when I was sure something AWESOME was about to happen. I loved that feeling.

True, every time I had felt it before, the awesome thing I was sure was about to happen turned out to be a HUGE DISAPPOINTMENT.

MAYBE.

But I was sure this time would be different. ←

"And as soon as I find where each part of the monster came from, I'll be able to build a new one," she went on. "And when I do, no one will ever compare me to my father again!"

"You mean, after you do the same thing he did?" I asked, confused. That didn't seem like the smartest idea to me. But I knew Fran was really clever. (Mostly because she kept telling me.)

"I've tried so many times to build my own monster," Fran explained. "I'm not going to say I failed, because a genius never fails. Those setbacks were a necessary part of the process. They showed me that there was something special about the parts that went into the original that made it work. I realized that to have any chance of recreating the monster, I would need to use the same genetic material. I could get that from the people whose body parts went into the original monster – if they were still alive. Bodies that have been dead for too long don't work. My other experiments proved that."

DNA

For some reason, I didn't want to ask what those other experiments were.

Yikes!

"But there's another possibility," she went on, scanning more pages from the journal. "I could use body parts that share the same DNA. The left arm from a relative of the original left arm. The right eye from a descendant of the monster's right eye. But the problem, of course, is finding those people."

"And then you turn up!" She smiled. "With my father's journal! He was a always writing things down. I'm sure that somewhere in his journal is all the information I need to track down every single living descendant of the people who went into his monster!"

"Once I use them to create a new monster, no one will ever compare me to my father again!" she exclaimed.

"You mean, after you do the same thing he did?" I asked again, still confused.

"Exactly!" she nodded, as if that explanation made perfect sense.

"But how are you going to do it?" I asked her. "I mean, I'm sure all those people are using their feet or eyes or whatever."

Fran just smiled a creepy little smile. And then I understood. Oh, no! No way!

She is crazy!

"Okay, wait. Hang on. You may be pretty," I said, and then wished I hadn't. "But I just found out that I have a family. I haven't even met them yet! I'm not going to let you use them for some kind of experiment!"

"It's not an experiment!" she roared. "I know it will work! Just like I know this will work…"

Fran pushed a button on the worktop next to her. And then I, the stool I was sitting on, my journal and the bowl of guacamole fell into darkness.

"WHOA!" I cried, falling down and out through an opening in the side of the house. **CLANG!** A metal flap slammed shut behind me as – **SQUOONCH!** – I landed in a pile of mouldy guacamole. My journal splashed down next to me. (GROSS!)

I picked it up and put it into my bag. I looked around and saw that I was in a small pen with a dog house.

Fran must have sent me down the shoot that she used to feed her dog!

But the thing that came out of the dog house was no dog. Or maybe it had been once. The awful BEAST was clearly one of her experiments.

It growled hungrily. Then, the "dog" opened its mouth (at least, I think it was its mouth) and leaped!

But not at me – at the fresh guacamole. As it gobbled it down, I climbed onto the stool, balanced on my big feet and jumped over the fence. I ran around the house and back inside through the open front door. But when I got to the kitchen door, I stopped short. What would Fran do to me?

I counted to three. And then four. And then FIVE. And then I charged into the kitchen! What I saw was even scarier than I had imagined. FRAN WAS GONE! And she had taken Dr Frankenstein's journal with her!

Chapter 4

The house was empty. Fran could have been anywhere by now. Well, not anywhere. She was probably heading straight for my family! I had to warn them. But I didn't know where – or even who – they were!

"Okay, don't panic," I told myself. "You'll work something out."

I looked around. On the computer screen were the pages of Dr Frankenstein's journal that she had scanned in. I could see they contained information about my dad and his body parts. I started printing the pages out.

But which body part was Fran after? She could be tracking down any one of them.

I took a deep breath and thought it through. She had left without closing the front door. She must have seen something that made her jump up and rush out. What could have made her do that?

I looked at the last thing she had scanned from the journal. It was a drawing of a pair of disgusting-looking feet. When I looked at those feet, I didn't feel disgusted. Instead I was shocked.

Those tiny toenails! The bumpy ankles. The feet in the drawing looked just like MY feet!

But there was something else that made my hair stand on end: The words scribbled on the bottom of the page. "Subject: Mr Percy of Victorville."

Mr Percy must have been the man my dad got his feet from!

Subject: Mr Percy of Victorville

I didn't even have to type the town or the man's name into Fran's computer. They were the last things in her search history. I clicked on the one article in the list that was highlighted in green, meaning it had already been read. It led to an article about Mr Percy, a famous explorer who lived in a small town called Victorville.

That must have been where Fran was heading right now!

I had to get there before she did and warn him! Even though I had no idea where Victorville was or how to get there.

As I jumped up to rush out, I accidentally hit the mouse and clicked on another link. It brought up an article that said that the famous explorer Mr Percy of Victorville had died many years ago (I hoped before Dr Frankenstein got his hands on his feet!).

I remembered what Fran had said: bodies that had been dead for too long were no use to her. So I sat down and did a little more digging.

It turned out that Mr Percy had a son. His name was Robert – and he was an explorer, too.

I printed out the most recent article I could find about him. It talked about Robert's expedition to an island in the South Pacific.

According to the story, Robert hadn't taken any of his high-tech exploring gear with him on this expedition. He had to use what he found. He lived on bananas, and used coconuts to mark his trail. Blah, blah, blah. That didn't really interest me.

But the photo did...

"'I lived on bananas and used coconuts to mark the right way to go,' said the explorer Robert Percy."

In it, Robert was barefoot. He had the same tiny toenails and the same bumpy ankles as me.

No doubt about it ... he was my cousin!

The article mentioned that an Explorers Club had sponsored Robert's trip. That was a couple of years ago. I couldn't find any more recent information on Robert, but a quick search revealed that the Explorers Club was right here in this town.

Fran didn't know any of this — it wasn't in her search history.

Which meant that while she was chasing a dead end (literally), I had a chance to find Robert before she did!

I took out my journal and wiped off the last bits of guacamole. There were still plenty of blank pages in it, so I taped in all of the scanned pages I had from Dr Frankenstein's journal, as well as the article about Robert.

Then I printed out a map of the town with the Explorers Club marked on it. I taped the map inside my journal, too.

That's when I realized: I had used Fran's computer to do all of this! She could probably work out how to retrieve my search, just like I had found her search!

Even if I tried to smash the computer or delete the search, someone as clever as Fran could probably work out a way to retrieve it.

But there was no time to worry about that. I had to get to Robert first! Grabbing my journal, I rushed to the door.

And then I stopped.

I ran back to the fridge, grabbed all the guacamole and dumped it down the leftovers chute. I didn't want the beast outside going hungry. I didn't know when Fran would come back. I just hoped that when she did, it would be without my cousin.

Chapter 5

Outside Fran's house, I opened my journal to the page with the map taped to it. In all the time I'd lived at the orphanage, I hadn't done much exploring. But I had a map. How hard could it be to find the Explorers Club?

Just as I stepped in some dog poo, taking a short cut through a park, I realized I must have made a mistake. And not by turning left when I should have turned right.

I mean, I must have made a mistake thinking I could be related to an explorer!

I was just about the opposite of an explorer. I couldn't find my way anywhere!

A couple of hours later, my feet were sore all the way from my bumpy ankles to my tiny toenails. But I had found the Explorers Club.

The building looked like a cross between an Egyptian pyramid, the Great Wall of China and an igloo. I supposed that every time one of the explorers got back from somewhere, they must've added something from that place to the building.

I pushed on the front door, which looked like it was from an Aztec temple.

CREEEAAK.

The door swung open.

the Explorers Club

Inside, the hallway was lined with huge paintings. A sign above them read "Past Members". One of the pictures showed an explorer being swallowed by quicksand. Another was of a man being mauled by a tiger in the jungle. The rest were even more gruesome.

HOPE HE'S OKAY!

At the end of the hallway, I heard voices coming from behind a door that looked a bit scary.

(It didn't smell all that great either.)

But there didn't seem to be anyone else in the whole building.

So I took a deep breath and pushed the door open.

Inside was a cloakroom, crowded with a group of very old men.

"I say," one of them said to me, "you're a little peculiar looking for an explorer."

"Oh, no, I'm not an explorer," I replied. "The front door was unlocked, so I just..."

The old men nodded.

"Hmm ... must have forgotten to lock that again," said one of them. "But then, we seem to be forgetting a lot of things these days. We were on our way to the dining room just now when we forgot the way and ended up here. Rather embarrassing for a group of explorers, wouldn't you say?"

I didn't know anything about exploring, or explorers, so I told them I really couldn't say.

"Anyway, it's nice to meet a young man with an interest in exploring," said a tall explorer.

"So tell us, where have you been?" said another. "Anywhere exotic? There's nothing explorers love more than a good tale of a trip to the exotic!"

The other explorers nodded excitedly as they crowded around me.

"Well, apart from Mr Shelley's orphanage," I told them, "the only place I've been is here."

They all looked disappointed.

"To be honest," I said, "before this morning, I didn't even know that there were still explorers. Well, except Dora –"

All the explorers let out a groan.

"Sorry," I said, embarrassed. "I know that's just a cartoon."

"Oh, no, that cartoon is based on a very real explorer," said the tall explorer. "Doratea Emma Maria is a member of this club. An excellent explorer. Just not as good an explorer as I am."

CRAZY HAIR!

"Or I!" said another.

"Or I!" echoed the rest.

"You know, those television people actually approached me first," said the tall explorer. "They wanted to make a cartoon about MY explorations. But I couldn't remember them!"

"Doratea always did have a good memory," said another explorer. "That's her strong point. That and her counting."

He turned to me. "Now then," he said. "What brings you here?"

I told him I was looking for an explorer called Robert Percy.

"Doesn't ring a bell," said the tall explorer. The other explorers murmured in agreement. My heart sank.

"No, wait!" said the tall explorer. "Now I remember. Robert is a member of this club. But he's not here at the moment."

Thank goodness! I'd found him!

Of course, I had to wait for him to come back. But I had waited my whole life to find my family. I could wait a little longer.

"When will he be back?" I asked.

The tall explorer looked at me. "Well, my best guess would be ... never."

Chapter 6

I stared at the tall explorer. I was sure I must have misheard him.

"Could you say that again?" I asked.

"Did you forget already?" He smiled. "Don't worry. Happens to me all the time. The explorer you're looking for is on a journey to the last unexplored part of Antarctica."

"An Antarctic explorer?" I spluttered, unable to think of anything else to say.

BRRRRR!

"Quite a mouthful, isn't it?" said the oldest explorer. "That's probably why there are so few of them."

"And now it seems there will be one less," the tall explorer said with a sigh.

"This is the last email we received from Robert," said the oldest explorer, taking a folded piece of paper from his jacket pocket. "Before all contact was lost with him. I can't remember how long ago it was."

"We keep forgetting to go after him," said the tall explorer. "Besides which, we are probably too old to do it anyway."

The others nodded sadly. Except for the oldest explorer. He smiled and pointed at me.

"But you're not old!" he shouted. "You're the youngest explorer here! You could rescue him! Here, take the email. It may help you."

He shoved the email into my hands.

"But I'm not an explorer," I reminded them. "I don't even know where Antarctica is! How would I even get there?"

None of the explorers had an answer for that.

"I'm heading that way," said a voice.

Everyone turned. Standing there in the open door to the cloakroom was a woman who was probably about thirty years old. Or maybe forty. (It's hard to tell when people get that old.)

"Doratea!" excalimed an explorer.

Doratea turned to me. She wore an old leather pilot's jacket over a purple shirt and orange trousers. A pair of flight goggles sat on top of her jet-black fringe.

"*Vamanos,*" she told me. "Let's go!"

*   *   *

BZZZZZZZZZZZ! I was trapped in a giant, buzzing blender that was shaking me to pieces.

I woke up from that dream to find myself being rattled in my seat as it bounced in the small cockpit of Doratea's seaplane. The buzzing came from the engines, which felt to me as though they were about to shudder the plane apart.

"You have slept for a while," said Doratea, her eyes fixed on the cockpit's window, or windscreen, or whatever you call it. "We are nearly there. I hope we are not too late. Roberto has not communicated in over a week. He may not have very much time left."

"He is my boyfriend," she added in a worried voice.

"How do you know Roberto?" she asked.

"Oh, I don't know him at all," I replied. "But he's my cousin."

I told her my story. (I left out a couple of the embarrassing parts.) It took a while. It would have been easier to just let her read my journal, but her hands and eyes were busy flying the plane.

Doratea smiled grimly when I finished my story. "I see," she said. "Well, it seems we both have very good reasons to want to rescue him. Luckily for us, I have this map!"

Doratea nodded at the map lying on the floor between us.

Her map! If it was anything like the map on the Dora cartoon, we'd definitely find my cousin!

"How does it talk?" I asked, grabbing the map and trying to find its mouth.

Doratea looked at me as though I had just picked my nose and offered her a taste.

"It doesn't talk," she replied. "It is a map."

"Oh," I nodded, not wanting to risk saying anything else that would sound so silly.

"But," she went on, "this map can still tell us many things. It's a copy of the map Roberto took with him on his expedition. Look."

"What do these symbols mean?" I asked.

"I don't know," replied Doratea. "Those dotted lines must be different paths Roberto considered. But I do not know which one he took. We will find out together, after we land."

"We are *muy circa* – very close," said Doratea. "Look..."

I looked out of the cockpit window. I knew I should have been impressed. But everything was just white.

"So this is Antarctica," I said, trying to sound excited.

"No," replied Doratea. "This is a cloud."

DUH!

She pushed down on the steering wheel or whatever you call the thing that steers a plane. As we nosed down, the engines rumbled louder and louder.

"This," shouted Doratea, "is Antarctica!"

Suddenly, there it was!

The snow was so bright in the sun it almost glowed. The whole thing looked like white icing on top of a cake.

It was the most beautiful continent I had ever seen.

As I stared down, I saw a ship, or whatever you call the kind of boat rich people own, sailing towards the shore. Doratea saw it too and shook her head.

"Scientific vessels travel here. Sometimes cruise ships. But private yachts like that one?" Doratea shook her head again. "That should not be here."

The yacht was too far away to see who was inside. But I knew. It was ...

YUMMMM!

Chapter 7

I quickly told Doratea all about Fran.

"I had planned for us to land and search for Roberto together," said Doratea. "But from what you say, I do not think we want this Señorita Kenstein to join us."

I definitely agreed with that.

"So we need a new plan," said Doratea. "How will we get to Roberto? First, I will drop you off with the map. Next, I will fly over the yacht to lead Señorita Kenstein away. Then, I will fly back and join you. And that's how we will get to Roberto."

"Now," she added, "are you ready to jump out of this aeroplane?"

I was too surprised by the question to answer.

"Great!" she nodded, as if I had said yes. "Count down with me ... *cinco, cuatro, tres, dos, uno, go!*"

"Wait, you want me to jump out of this plane right now?!" I exclaimed.

"No, I wanted you to do it when I told you to GO!" she replied. "But now will have to do."

With one sharp kick, Doratea shoved me out of the plane with her boot.

"Stay where you land. I will meet you as soon as I draw Señorita Kenstein away!" she yelled as I fell. "*Hasta luego, amigo!*"

At least, that's what I think she said. I was too busy looking at the white ground rushing up towards me.

A hot jolt of panic spread down my arms.

It warmed the inside of the coat the explorers had given me, even though I was falling through air that was far below freezing.

WHOOOMP! Suddenly, I got a mouthful of snow as I fell face first onto the ground. But Doratea had brought me in just low enough. I was okay.

I got to my feet. From where I was standing, all I could see was snow and ice.

As I tried to think of what to do, a loud, rattling noise kept distracting me. I looked around for where that noise was coming from. And then I realized it was my teeth chattering.

I was

Just as I was starting to feel sorry for myself, I remembered my cousin. He had been lost out here for who knew how long.

If I was freezing, he was probably feeling worse.

A lot worse.

I opened my journal to where I had stuffed the copy of Robert's map. There were several different paths traced on it. I had no idea which one Robert had taken. I also didn't know how long it would take Doratea to come back. If I waited for her to start looking, it could be a long time before we found him.

I didn't know if he had that long.

Each path was marked with a different symbol – a pickaxe, a pile of coconuts, a water bottle. I didn't know what they meant. And yet, there was something familiar. But what? If one of the symbols was reminding me of something I'd seen, there was probably a clue on one of the pages of my journal.

And that's when it hit me. Robert's email! Doratea had arrived just after the explorer had handed it to me at the club. Things had been so rushed, I had shoved it into my journal and forgotten all about it. It had to have the clue I needed.

My hands were shaking with excitement (or maybe frostbite) as I read it:

HULLO FELLOW EXPLORERS CLUB MEMBERS!

I can't be sure when you will remember to check your email, so I may already be safely back at home by the time you read this.

Tomorrow, I'll be leaving the Eastern Antarctic Research Station, on my trek to the last unexplored spot on this beautiful continent. It should only take me a day or so to get there.

The hard part is finding the right path to take. But that's exactly what I've done! To celebrate, I'm sending you this photo as I set out on my historic journey!

Cheerio!

Robert

Robert was holding a glass of champagne in the photo. Was that the clue I was looking for? On his map, one of the paths was marked with a water bottle. That wasn't exactly a glass of champagne, but it was pretty close!

I raced to follow that path. With my big feet, it was almost like having a pair of snowshoes, and I made good time across the snow. Pretty soon, I came across some footprints. I'd done it!

Yep, I'd done it all right – I had managed to get myself completely lost!

The footprints I had found were mine. Somehow, I had got turned around and criss-crossed my own tracks. I wasn't on the right path. The champagne glass in the photo hadn't been a clue after all.

And just as I realized that I had no idea where I was, it started to snow. Heavily.

"Don't panic," I told myself. "You'll work something out." But all I could think was: what was I thinking?

I was no explorer! I had trouble following a map to get across my own town! Which it looked like I'd probably never see again.

I didn't know how far I was from where Doratea told me to wait for her. I'd probably freeze before she could find me.

A **WHOOSH** of wind and ice ripped past me.

I may not have been an explorer,
but I knew a blizzard when I felt one.

Snow poured down on my journal, soaking the pages.

I knew what I had to do. I wrapped up my journal
as carefully as I could and buried it deep in the snow.
Maybe someone else would find it and the map –
someone who could work out which object marked the
right way to go.

UGH

Chapter 8

Marked the right way to go! That was it! That was what I had remembered!

I dug up the journal as quickly as I could. In the article, I read about Robert's trip to the tropical island ... Yes! There it was!

When Robert had explored the island, he had used coconuts to mark the right way to go!

"'I lived on bananas and used coconuts to mark the right way to go,' said the explorer Robert Percy."

I opened the map. One of the dotted lines was marked with coconuts! That had to be the right path.

I had been right that the clue I needed was on one of the pages in my journal. I just picked the wrong page before.

It stopped snowing as I followed the coconut path on the map. It led me up a large mound of snow that gave me a view of the icy shore.

And that's where I saw Robert, bobbing up and down in the water.

His lower half was covered by a fridge-sized block of ice. His head and chest stuck out of the top of the ice block, allowing him to breath. But his arms and legs were pinned inside the chunk of ice. He was trapped.

I couldn't believe it. I'd done it! I'd found him! I'd had to come all the way to Antarctica, but I'd finally found a member of my family!

I raced down the other side of the mound, straight towards Robert.

As I ran, I thought of what I would say to him. I wanted to make a good first impression for once. So I tried to think of just the right thing to say to break the ice.

But then ... the ice broke!

"**WHHHULP!**" I cried as the sheet of ice I was running down cracked and sent me sliding on my back with my legs in the air.

I clutched at the ice around me, but it was too slippery. I couldn't stop myself.

I was heading feet first right towards the freezing water.

"Hullo there!" shouted Robert cheerily as I slid towards him. "Not to be a bother, but you had better stop yourself before you splash in here, or I dare say you'll end up an ice cube lIke me! How about putting your huge clodhoppers to good use!"

"**MY WHAT**?" I shouted.

"Your large feet," said Robert. "Put them down to get some traction."

I put my feet flat against the ice. I started to slow down. I stopped right at the water's edge.

"Thanks!" I gasped.

"Jolly good of the old boys at the club to finally send an explorer to rescue me," said Robert. "Even if you are a bit of a peculiar-looking one."

"I get my looks from my dad," I told him proudly. "But I'm no explorer."

I quickly told him my whole story.

I told him everything I'd written in here up to now (even the embarrassing parts – he was family, after all). I told him how I teamed up with Doratea so I could find him, because I was the son of Frankenstein's Monster and was looking for my family. I told him how I was related to him through his father's feet. "Which makes you my cousin," I said.

Robert just looked at me. The only sound was the lapping of the water on the ice.

That's when I realized how crazy I must have sounded. I had just come halfway around the world (Or was it more than that? I didn't even know!) to find him. And now he wouldn't even believe we were related!

There was only one thing to do. I started to take off my boots.

"What are you doing?" he asked.

"I want to show you my feet!" I said. "I can prove we're related!"

He just looked at me, even more confused. "My dear boy, why would you do that?" he asked. "Of course we're related!"

"The very first person to ever find his way to this place was me." He smiled proudly. "You, my boy, are the second. If that doesn't prove you've got the blood of an explorer in you, I don't know what will!"

I didn't think I could feel any happier than I felt right then. Until I heard the familiar **RMMMMMM** of Doratea's plane circling over the water!

Minutes later, the seaplane splashed down in the water off shore. **CRUNK!** The cockpit door popped open and a rubber raft flopped out.

But Doratea didn't jump out of the plane and onto the raft.

Fran did!

OH NO!

Chapter 9

"**HHHHRRUNH!**" I grunted as I tried to pull Robert out of the water. The block of ice probably weighed five-hundred kilograms. And I had to be careful not to slip, or else I'd end up like an ice lolly too.

It was no use. And Fran was getting closer.

"Where's Doratea?" Robert shouted at her. "What did you do to her?"

"Not as much as I would have liked," said Fran with a creepy smile. "She had a surprising number of items in that little purple rucksack of hers."

"Creepy Smile"

"But no matter," continued Fran as she paddled closer. "I left your friend floating in the ocean. She cannot help you now."

I stopped pulling. There was no way I was going to get Robert out of the water. And even if I did, it wasn't as though I could carry him in that block of ice.

But there was no way I was leaving him. Not after waiting my whole life to find him.

There was only one thing to do. Just as Fran's raft hit the shore, I leaped at the water ... and landed on Robert's block of ice! Bracing myself with my big feet, I didn't slide off. Instead, my momentum pushed us out to sea.

Right towards the plane!

"Well done!" exclaimed Robert.

Fran growled and raced after us in her raft.

I stuck my big feet into the water and kicked.

We had a head start, but she was gaining on us.

"When we get to the plane, you won't be able
to get me inside like this," Robert said matter-of-
factly. I suppose to an explorer being used as a boat
while being chased by the crazy daughter of Dr
Frankenstein wasn't anything to get too worked up
about. "You'll have to tie me to one of the pontoons."

Fran was just a few metres behind us when we
reached the plane. I flung open the cockpit door and
climbed in, my feet instantly turning to ice cubes as
soon as I took them out of the water.
I quickly found a rope. But as I tied
Robert's block to the pontoon, I
suddenly realized: "Wait! Who's
going to fly the plane!?!"

"You are!" he said cheerily.

"Me?" I cried. "I don't know how! There's no way I
can fly a plane!"

"It's the duty of explorers to go where people think they cannot," said Robert. "Even if the people who think that are the explorers themselves!"

Fran was right there, reaching with a knife to cut Robert loose. I didn't know which button to push. So I pushed them all. The windscreen wipers wiped. The wing flaps flapped. The lights lit up.

And then, I just about heard Fran cursing me as the engine roared to life and drowned her out.

Wooooooo!

A couple of days later, I got an email from Robert.

FROM: ROBERT.PERCY@EXPLORERS.NET
TO:< JD@EXPLORERS.NET>
SUBJECT: HULLO!

Hullo cousin!

Just landed the plane to refuel at the research station and found a computer I could borrow for a few minutes. I've been searching day and night since I dropped you on the mainland. No luck finding Doratea yet, but I know I will.

Despite the fantastic escape we made, I can tell Ms Kenstein isn't the type who will just give up and call it a day. Now that I know to look out for her, I'm confident I can throw a spanner in the works if she comes after me again.

But you need to warn the rest of your cousins before Ms Kenstein can find them. I'm certain you will, even if you have to go to the ends of the Earth to do so.

You've got the blood of an explorer in you, just like me. When adventure calls, you go feet first!

But you already know that. What I wanted to tell you is that I have never been on an adventure like the one I had with you. My father died before I was old enough to go exploring with him. This was my first adventure with family.

But not the last. As soon as I find Doratea, I plan to join you on your quest to find the rest of your family. And by that time, Doratea will be family too – the first thing I'm going to do when I see her is ask her to marry me.

I hope you're chuffed about this news, old boy! You thought you had only found one cousin so far, but you've actually met two!

Cheerio!

Robert

I had a big smile on my face as I taped Robert's email to a blank page in my journal.

It was still a little cold and soggy from the Antarctic waters, but all the pages I had from Dr Frankenstein's journal were still inside.

And somewhere out there, Fran was looking for the rest of my cousins. But I knew nothing bad would happen to them ...

Because I was going to find them First!

GLOSSARY

Antarctic area around the South Pole

descendants person's children, their children, and so on into the future

DNA molecule that carries the genetic code that gives living things their special characteristics

expedition long journey for a special purpose such as exploring

momentum force or speed that an object has when it is moving

neglected failed to take care of someone or something

orphanage place where orphans live and are looked after

residence place where somebody lives

NOT AS SCARY AS HE LOOKS!

Scott Sonneborn has written several books, one script for a circus performance (for Ringling Bros. and Barnum & Bailey) and many TV series. He's been nominated for one Emmy award and spent three very cool years working at DC Comics. He lives in California, USA, with his wife and their two sons.

COOLEST ILLUSTRATOR EVER!

Timothy Banks is an award-winning illustrator known for his ability to create magically quirky illustrations for children and adults. He has a Master of Fine Arts degree in Illustration, and he also teaches art students in his spare time. Timothy lives in South Carolina, USA, with his wonderful wife, two beautiful daughters and two crazy pugs.

Read the next book in the
Frankenstein Journals series...

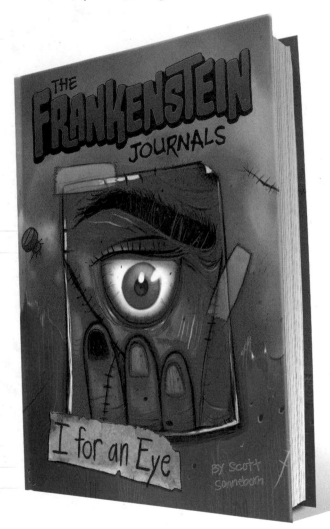